Career Day

story by **Anne Rockwell**   pictures by **Lizzy Rockwell**

HarperCollins*Publishers*

Career Day • Text copyright © 2000 by Anne Rockwell • Illustrations copyright © 2000 by Lizzy Rockwell • Printed in the U.S.A.   All rights reserved.
Visit our web site at http://www.harperchildrens.com. • Library of Congress Cataloging-in-Publication Data • Rockwell, Anne F. • Career day / story by
Anne Rockwell ; pictures by Lizzy Rockwell.   p.   cm.   Summary: Each child in Mrs. Madoff's class brings a visitor who tells the group about his or
her job.   ISBN 0-06-027565-0. — ISBN 0-06-027566-9 (lib. bdg.)   [1. Schools—Fiction.   2. Occupations—Fiction.]   I. Rockwell, Lizzy, ill.   II. Title.
PZ7.R5943 Car   2000   97-20999   [E]—DC21   CIP AC   Typography by Elynn Cohen 1   2   3   4   5   6   7   8   9   10 ❖ First Edition

For Christian and Sam,
who will grow up to do something wonderful.
—A.R. and L.R.

When special visitors come to our school,
they tell us about the work they do.
Then we tell them about the work we do.
Today it's my turn to introduce my visitor.

Jessica CALENDAR

Sam JUICE

Michiko LEADER

Charlie LIGHTS

Nicholas WEATHER

Kate PLANTS

Eveline SNACK

Pablo FLUFFY

Evan RS

Sarah MAIL

What if I forget what I'm supposed to say?
Sometimes that happens.
Not just to me, Mrs. Madoff says,
but to everyone.

Here he is—right on time!
"Uh, this is my dad," I say.
"He drives a big bulldozer.
He's helping build our new library."
"Good morning, Mr. Lopez," everyone says.
"Good morning, boys and girls," my dad says.

Next we meet Charlie's visitor.
His mother is a judge who works
in a courtroom and wears a long black robe.
If there's too much noise, she pounds her gavel
and says, "Order in the court!"
Then everyone has to be quiet.

When Kate introduces her visitor, she says, "My dad plays bass in an orchestra at night. He practices all day and takes care of my baby brother while our mother goes to work at the bank."

Michiko's mother writes books for us to read.
She draws the pictures in them, too.
She is very good at drawing mice.

Mrs. Madoff's visitor is her husband.
He's a scientist called a paleontologist.
He just got back from South America,
where he was digging for dinosaur bones.
The bones tell us about dinosaurs
that lived long ago.

Sarah's visitor is our crossing guard.
She brings Sarah to school every day,
because she is also Sarah's grandmother.
That's why Sarah is always the first one at school
and the last one to go home in the afternoon.

Eveline's mother is a nurse in the hospital.
She takes care of all the newborn babies in our town.
She tells us those babies are very, very cute,
but they sure do cry a lot when they're hungry.

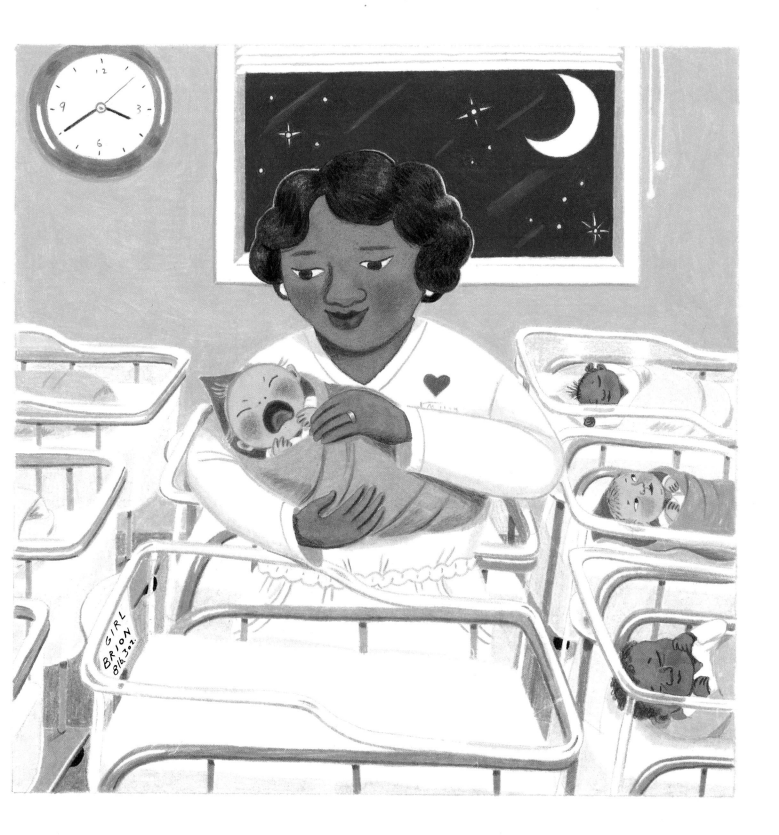

Jessica's mother takes care of animals. She's a veterinarian, the kind of doctor who makes sick animals better.

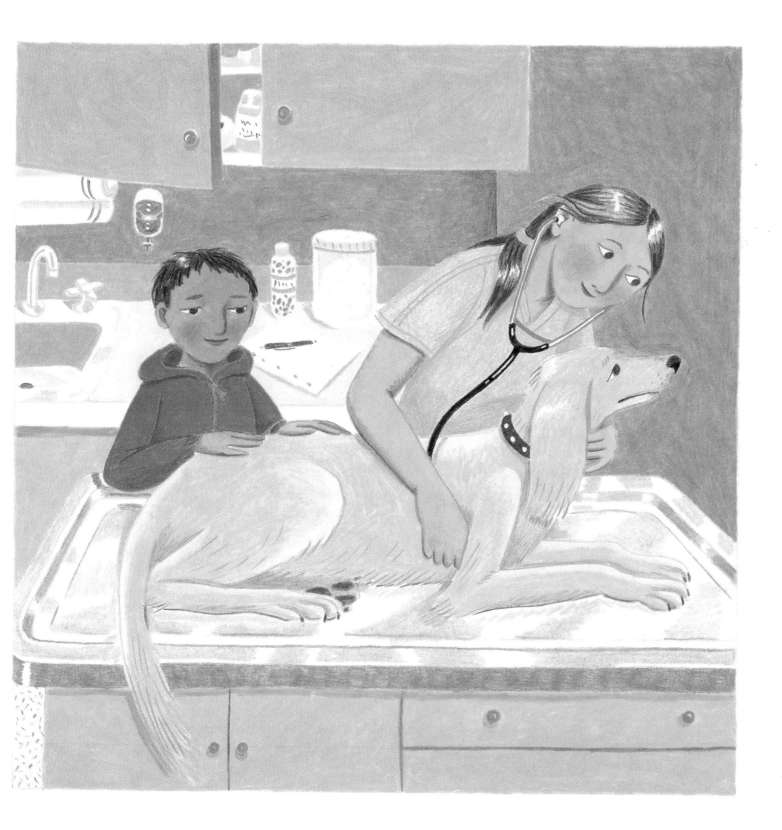

Sam's visitor drives the sanitation truck
that carries our garbage to the big town dump.
Kate and Eveline and I wave to him, just as
we always do whenever he comes down our street.
"Hey, kids—remember to recycle!" Sam's father says.

Evan's father wears a leather apron
that holds the tools he uses all the time.
He shows us how to hammer a nail.

When it's time for Nicholas
to introduce his visitor, he says,
"I'll bet you've all bought groceries
at the Friendly Farm Market.
Guess what—my father is manager of the store."

Today it's Mr. Siscoe's turn
to introduce his special visitor.
He says, "Good morning, everyone.
I'd like you to meet Professor Alcorn.
He's my teacher at college."
Hey—I never knew grown-ups
had teachers, too!

Jessica	PLANTS	Sam	WEATHER
Michiko	LIGHTS	charlie	CHAIRS
Nicholas	CALENDAR	kate	MAIL
Eveline	FLUFFY	Pablo	LEADER
Evan	JUICE	Sarah	SNACK

POCO

Grown-ups sure have interesting work to do!
And so do we.

I wonder what I'll be when I grow up.